MR GUM

and the
Dancing Bear

Shabba me whiskers! Andy Stanton's **MR GUM** is winner of the Roald Dahl Funny Prize, the Red House Children's Book Award AND the Blue Peter Book Award for The Most Fun Story With Pictures. AND he's been shortlisted for LOADS of other prizes too! It's barking bonkers!

PRAISE FOR **MR GUM**:

'Do not even think about buying another book – This is gut-spillingly funty.' Alex, aged 13

'It's hilarious, it's brilliant . . . Stanton's the Guv'nor, The Boss.' Danny Baker, BBC London Radio

'Funniest book I have ever and will ever read . . . When I read this to my mum she burst out laughing and nearly wet herself . . . When I had finished the book I wanted to read it all over again it was so good.' Bryony, aged 8

'Funny? You bet.' Guardian

'Andy Stanton accumulates silliness and jokes in an irresistible, laughter-inducing romp.' Sunday Times

'Raucous, revoltingly rambunctious and nose-snortingly funny.' Daily Mail

'David Tazzyman's illustrations match the irreverent sparks of word wizardry with slapdash delight.' Junior Education

'This is weird, wacky and one in a million.' Primary Times

'It provoked long and painful belly laughs from my daughter, who is eight.' Daily Telegraph

'As always, Stanton has a ball with dialogue, detail and devilish plot twists.' Scotsman

'We laughed so much it hurt.' Sophie, aged 9

'You will laugh so much you'll ache in places you didn't know you had.' First News

'A riotous read.' Sunday Express

'It's utterly bonkers and then a bit more – you'll love every madcap moment.' TBK Magazine

'Chaotically crazy.' Jewish Chronicle

'Designed to tickle young funny bones.' Glasgow Herald

'A complete joy to read whatever your age.' This is Kids' Stuff

'The truth is a lemon meringue!' Friday O'Leary

'They are brilliant.' Zoe Ball, Radio 2

'Smooky palooki! This book is well brilliant.' Jeremy Strong

'They're the funniest books . . . I can't recommend them enough.' Stephen Mangan

Mr Gum and the Dancing Bear
First published 2008 by Egmont UK Limited
This edition published 2019 by Egmont UK Limited,
The Yellow Building,1 Nicholas Road
London W11 4AN

Text copyright © 2008 Andy Stanton
Illustration copyright © 2008 David Tazzyman

The moral rights of the author and illustrator have been asserted

ISBN 978 1 4052 9373 0

mrgum.co.uk
www.egmont.co.uk

A CIP catalogue record for this title is available from the British Library
Printed and bound in Great Britain by the CPI Group

45110/001

MR GUM

and the Dancing Bear

ANDY STANTON

Illustrated by David Tazzyman

EGMONT

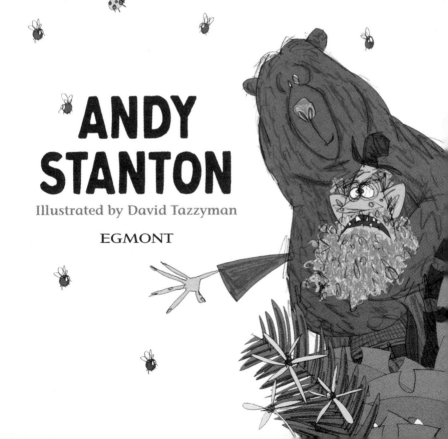

Read all of Andy Stanton's books!

You're a Bad Man, **MR GUM**!

MR GUM and the Biscuit Billionaire

MR GUM and the Goblins

MR GUM and the Power Crystals

MR GUM and the Dancing Bear

What's for Dinner, **MR GUM**?

MR GUM and the Cherry Tree

MR GUM and the Secret Hideout

Contents

Some of the crazy old townsfolk from Lamonic Bibber

Mrs Lovely

Friday O'Leary

Billy William the Third

Old Granny

Mr Gum

Martin Launderette

Alan Taylor

Polly

Chapter 1
Padlock the Bear

Who likes bears? Everyone likes bears. I likes bears, you likes bears, this guy I know called Will Bulman likes bears. Everyone likes bears. They are truly the king of the jungle. They are nature's way of saying, 'here's what bears look like'. They are the best. They are the bears.

And guess what, bear-likers? You're in luck, because this story is all about a bear. Not just any bear, mind you, but a startlingly big and handsome specimen who came strolling into the little town of Lamonic Bibber one fine autumn morning. He was a proper fat shaggy rumble-me-tumble sort of a roly-poly flip-flap-flopper of a big brown bear, not like some of these cheap bears you see nowadays who have hardly got any legs and need batteries.

He was as tall as two men, or about forty hamsters if you could only manage to glue them on top of each other to prove it. And he weighed as much as two hundred watermelons, or roughly nineteen thousand grapes.

But what about his fur? Well, I'm glad I asked me that because he was covered from head to foot in the most gorgeous, chocolate-coloured fur you've ever seen. It was soft and deep and long, and it was glossy with healthy goodness, just like a bear's fur should be. And his eyes, oh his eyes, his precious hazel eyes! One look into those big beautiful blinkers and that was it, you were in love forever.

And as this glorious new arrival came

4

rumbling down the high street on his thick hind legs, everyone stopped what they were doing to stare.

'Kroola-hoola!' exclaimed Jonathan Ripples, the fattest man in town. 'He's as fat as me!'

'Wab!' remarked Old Granny, the oldest woman in Lamonic Bibber. 'There hasn't been a bear in this town since the Great Gecko Plague of 1922 – and even then there weren't any bears, just quite a lot of geckos.'

'A bear!' shouted the postman.

'A bear!' shouted the milkman.

'Hey, you greedy herons! Keep away from my breakfast!' shouted Friday O'Leary, who was having a spot of bother over at the *Heron Attack Café*.

Soon there was a huge parade of laughing

townsfolk, all capering and cavorting along behind the lumbering bear as he waddled down the high street and into the town square. And there, upon a bench beneath the statue of Sir Henry Violin, the inventor of the saxophone, the bear sat himself down, buried his face in his paws and began to sob.

Well now. There is nothing quite as sad as the sight of a sobbing bear. It is sadder than a broken toy lying in the rain. It is sadder than a little white onion being bullied by a gang of tough courgettes in leather jackets. It is sadder than a grandma who no one comes to visit because her face is just too hairy. Believe me, children of all ages, a sobbing bear is not a happy sight.

The townsfolk looked on in astonishment. But did any of them go and comfort that poor beast in his hour of soggy need? No, they did not. Oh, they all *said* they liked bears. They all donated money to charities like 'Bear Aid', 'Save The Bears' and 'Let's Buy Some Bears a New Toothbrush'. But when it came to actually helping one out in real life, it was another story entirely. It was a story of the townsfolk looking on in astonishment – until a heroic young girl called Polly passed by, that is. Polly was nine years old, with lovely sandy hair and nice trainers, and she simply couldn't stand to see another person in trouble, especially if that person happened to be a bear.

'My goodnesses, that's not right,' she

exclaimed, and without a thought for her own safety she approached the beast as he sat there, bawling away like a greengrocer.

'Good morning, furry visitor,' said Polly. 'I'm sorry you're so sad.'

'Mmmmmph?' said the bear, for the truth was that no human being had ever spoken so kindly to him before. Taking his tear-stained paws from his eyes, he peered at the little girl who stood unafraid before him in the bright autumn sunshine.

'Eat her! Eat her! Eat her!' chanted the townsfolk. Not really, but it would have been funny if they had.

'My name's Polly,' said Polly, gazing into the creature's doleful hazel eyes. Through his tears the bear gazed back at Polly, and in that moment something remarkable happened. In that moment the two of them became the best of friends, like Laurel & Hardy or Batman & Robin or Albert Einstein & Tarzan.

'I'm a-gonna call you "Padlock",' Polly told the bear, 'if that's OK with you. Do you like crackers? I got loads in my skirt pocket, only some of them's a bit broken, sorry.'

But Padlock didn't mind at all, and together he and Polly sat in the town square eating broken crackers while all around them the leaves fell, soft and sad like autumn's teardrops.

Chapter 2

The World Champion
of the Butcher's Shop
Lying Contest

But where were those outrageous tinklers, Mr Gum and Billy William the Third, while all this was going on? Well, they were loafing around Billy William's unhygienic butcher's shop, scoffing rancid entrails by the bucketful and having a contest to see who could tell the most lies in one minute. Mr Gum was in the lead with eleven monstrous untruths but now it was Billy's turn and he was raring to go.

'On yer marks . . . get set . . . LIE YER FLIPPIN' EYEBROWS OFF!' shouted Mr Gum, starting up a stopwatch in his mean old hand – and Billy leapt into action.

'Right,' he began, screwing his ears up with concentration, 'I'm the President of Space! I'm over six hundred years old! I . . . um . . . I once done a drawin' of a crocodile so brilliant it came to life an' bit me legs off . . . '

'SUPER-FIB BONUS!' shouted Mr Gum, spitting entrails all over Billy's face in his excitement. 'Two lies in one!'

'Um . . . ,' said Billy, 'I got a car what's so fast it keeps drivin' into the future! I got five arms! I don't smell! There's a secret world hidden under my cap! I once kissed a lady! I sell only the finest quality meats in my shop . . . um . . . '

'Time up!' growled Mr Gum suddenly, which was a lie in itself as Billy still had fifteen seconds to go. 'Unlucky, Billy me old nozzler, it was a good try but you only got ten lies.

So I'm still the reignin' World Champion Liar of the Butcher's Shop!'

'Here, let me see that stopwatch,' said Billy William suspiciously but Mr Gum quickly smashed it to bits on the counter and ate the pieces.

'What stopwatch?' said Mr Gum innocently, a spring hanging out of his mouth.

Well, a fight might have broken out just then, but at that moment Mr Gum happened to glance out the fly-covered window. And when he saw what was going on outside in the town square, his eyes lit up like razor blades.

'Hang on, Billy me boy,' he exclaimed. 'At long last our luck's changin' for the better. See that bear out there? Well, he's our ticket to fame, fortune, glory, some more fame, riches, wealth an' a bit more fortune.'

'How's that then?' enquired Billy William, squashing a fly against the windowpane and drawing a big question mark on the glass with its blood. 'He's only a stinkin' bear!'

'Yeah, but wait 'til we get 'im *dancin'* for us!' scowled Mr Gum happily. 'Everyone loves a dancin' bear – an' they'll pay anythin' to see it! The bear dances, you go 'round with a hat to collect up the cash an' I sit back on a comfy chair shoutin', "Oi, Billy! Bring me all that money or I'll kick ya in the ribs!" Yes,' laughed Mr Gum, 'once we get our hands on that bear, it's riches all the way for us, 'specially me. An' that ain't no lie!'

Chapter 3

What's to Be Done with Padlock the Bear?

And so the days passed as autumn wore on in that gusty, blustery way that it does. In the butcher's shop, Mr Gum and Billy William sat making their plans. In the cake shop, the baker sat making his flans. And in the town square, Polly sat with Padlock, wringing her hands.

'Oh, Padlock,' sighed Polly worriedly. 'Every day I bring you crackers an' tell you jokes to cheer you up, but nothin's a-workin'. What's wrong, boy?'

Padlock's only answer was a tired little 'mmph'. He seemed unhappier than ever. He was growing thinner by the day, and his big hazel eyes were empty and lifeless, like a boarded-up cinema in a town called Misery. Often he hardly even seemed to notice Polly, but just gazed mournfully off into the distance, rocking back and forth all the while.

Worst of all was his fur. Not only had it lost its lovely rich glossiness – it was actually starting to fall out. Every morning Polly would find more of Padlock's fur on the ground and less of Padlock's fur on Padlock, until one day she could take it no more.

'I'm gonna visit Alan Taylor,' Polly told

Padlock as he sat there sobbing and not even bothering to wipe his runny nose with his paws. 'He's a brilliant headmaster what knows all 'bout the natural world. Maybe *he* can help you.'

'Polly!' beamed Alan Taylor when she turned up on the steps of Saint Pterodactyl's School For The Poor later that afternoon. 'What a delightful surprise!'

'Hello,' said Polly, bending down to give him a hug. She had to bend down because Alan Taylor was only 15.24 centimetres tall. He was probably the world's smallest ever headmaster, and almost definitely the only one to be made out of gingerbread. His electric muscles sparked and whirred merrily as he led Polly along a long corridor lined with drawings done by the schoolchildren. Even the rubbish drawings were pinned up, because Alan Taylor wasn't the kind of headmaster who says things like, 'Blimey, this drawing's pathetic, is that supposed to be a tree?' He was the kind of headmaster who says things like, 'Well done for trying, have a gold star and some sweets.'

'Well now, Polly,' said Alan Taylor when they were seated comfortably in the soft leather chairs in his headmaster's study. 'What brings you here today?'

So Polly told the little biscuit all about Padlock.

'An' I thought you might know what's wrong

with him, Alan Taylor, 'cos you're such a professor of the natural world,' she finished, gazing in awe at all the books on the bookshelves. There were five in all, and they were titled: 'ANIMALS A–G', 'ANIMALS H–L', 'ANIMALS M–Q', 'ANIMALS R–Y' and 'ZEBRAS'.

'Hmm,' said Alan Taylor, leaning back in his chair and taking a puff on a tiny liquorice pipe. 'Would you mind handing me that copy of "ANIMALS A–G", Polly? I think we might find what we're looking for in there.'

So Polly took down the heavy book, which was bigger than Alan Taylor himself, and she turned the pages until she came to the section about bears.

'Let's see,' said Alan Taylor, jumping on to the page for a better look. 'Hmm . . . interesting . . . aha! Just as I thought,' he nodded. 'Padlock is showing all the signs of homesickness. You see, Polly, bears are not meant to be cooped up in the World of Men. They simply aren't born to drive cars, or to work in shoe shops – or even to sit around town squares doing nothing all day long. If you ask me,' continued the headmaster, 'Padlock's real home is the Kingdom of the Beasts, where he can roam wild and free and hairy as nature intended.'

'Oh, thank you, Alan Taylor, thank you,' said Polly gratefully. 'I knewed you'd have the answer! I'll go an' put things right at once. But will you help me?' she asked hopefully, because Alan

Taylor was always good to have along on adventures, and whenever he fell asleep you could secretly nibble his delicious gingerbread fingernails.

Alan Taylor sighed.

'I'd love to, Polly, but I just can't. I've got a huge pile of essays to mark and it's Parents' Evening next week. It's quite hard work being a headmaster, you know.'

'Well, you're the best one what I ever heard

of,' said Polly, giving her friend a lovely big kiss on the nose. And bidding Alan Taylor a fond farewell she set off to see about returning Padlock to the Kingdom of the Beasts where he belonged.

Chapter 4

The Baddies, the Bear and the Balloon

*B*ack in the town square the autumn evening is drawing in. The last of the light is fading from the sky like a television being switched off for the night, and a cold wind has blown up, rustling the leaves at Padlock's feet and making the squirrels in the treetops shiver so hard the hazelnuts fall out of their pockets. But Padlock the bear is so sad that he doesn't notice the cold, or the wind that riffles his fur, or the way the statues in the town square almost seem to be moving in the gathering gloom . . .

🍃 🍃 🍃

'Shabba me whiskers,' whispers one of the statues, a scruffy figure with a big red beard sitting astride a statue of a horse. 'We been standin' totally still like this for over a week, waitin' for our chance. I'm completely sick of it an' my nose is startin' to itch.'

'Patience, me old dressin' gown,' replies his horse, who looks surprisingly like a grubby old butcher. 'Not much longer now.'

The statues wait there a while longer until the last passer-by has passed by. And then, when at last no one else is around –

'NOW!' yells the horse, and the statues

STATUE

spring to life, jumping down from their pedestal and running towards the startled bear at the speed of villains.

'That's for makin' me pretend to be a statue all week, you useless mammal!' snarls Mr Gum, kicking Padlock in the bottom with his hobnail boot.

'Look at his stupid fur falling out all over the place,' laughs Billy, tearing out a handful of the stuff with his unkind fists. 'It's funty!'

'Yeah,' agrees Mr Gum. 'An' jus' you wait 'til we set 'im to dancin', Billy! We'll both be filthy stinkin' rich, apart from you. You'll jus' be filthy an' stinkin'.'

Chuckling nastily, the villains drag the weakened, terrified Padlock away to his new life of dancing around like a washing line. And by the time Polly returns to the square Padlock is nowhere to be found.

'Oh, GURKLES!' cursed Polly, rushing over to the bench and feeling about on it just in case Padlock was still there but had turned invisible, like bears sometimes do. But no – he had really gone.

'What am I a-gonna do now?' she sighed. 'I done left Padlock all alone in the World of Men with no one to protect him an' now he could be in all sorts of troubles. I let that big bear down pure an' simple. I'm a disgracer to the name of nine-year-olds!'

The autumn wind sighed softly, scattering the leaves which lay fallen in deep drifts upon the ground. Scattering them to reveal –

'Paw prints!' cried Polly. 'Padlock done made brilliant clues with his feet to help me track him down!'

Soon she was hot on the trail, following the muddy marks as they led her through the flower beds and out of the town square. Out of the town

square and down the high street. Down the high street and on past Shakyhand McClumsy's, the best barber shop in town. Past Shakyhand McClumsy's and through the little backstreets. Through the backstreets and over the railway tracks. Over the railway tracks and . . . but there the trail ended. There was so much rubbish and muck on the ground that Polly couldn't make out the paw prints in the fading light.

'Which way now?' she said in frustration. 'It's impossible to tell, that's what!'

But just at that
moment there
came a voice
and it was
calling, calling,
calling from the

heavens above, it was calling, calling, calling
from the heavens above, yeah, it was calling from
the heavens above.

'Look at me, Polly, look at me!' called the
voice, and Polly was flabbergasted to see a splendid
red hot-air balloon sailing through the sky, with
the words **FLAVOURS OF DISCOVERY**
painted on the side in letters of green and gold.

And standing in the basket, fiddling with a yellow rope which had got tangled up in his chins, was none other than Jonathan Ripples, the fattest man in town.

'Huzzoo!' yelled he, 'huzzoo, huzzay! I'm bored of the snacks we've got here in Lamonic Bibber – I'm off around the world to try out new ones! Who knows what wonderful delicacies I'll discover?' he laughed, his eyes shining and his stomach rumbling like a whopper. 'But, Polly,' he exclaimed as he noticed how unhappy she looked. 'Whatever's the matter?'

'It's Padlock,' replied Polly. 'I done lost him by accident.'

'Well, maybe I can help,' said Jonathan Ripples, scanning the streets spread out below him like a big moving map. 'Yes, there's your bear. He's heading towards the docks. But be careful, Polly – he's not alone!'

'What do you mean?' said Polly, but already

her heart had guessed at the awful truth.

'It's Mr Gum and Billy William!' yelled Jonathan Ripples as the balloon rose higher on the warm evening air. 'They're the ones who've got Padlock!'

'So they're behinds it, I might have known,' trembled Polly. 'Thank you, Mr Ripples, sir!' she called after the disappearing balloon.

And with the smell of calamity whistling through her ribcage, Polly raced along the shabby winding lane that led down to the Lamonic Bibber docks.

Chapter 5
Down by the Docks

The docks! Where life was cheap and death was on special offer all year round. Where danger lurked around every corner, and each step you took might be your last.

Where a man could lose an entire month's pay in five minutes gambling for cheese with the rats in the gutters, and the sailors sang drunken, and the clocks were all broken, and the barrels of rum hulked menacingly in the fog, and you never knew what anyone was thinking, but one thing was for certain – you knew they wished you harm.

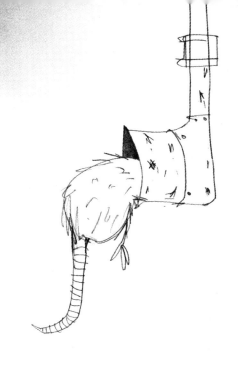

Cautiously Polly picked her way through the narrow lanes lit dimly by Victorian gas lamps that glowed a dismal orange through the swirling mists. The air was thick with salt and exotic spices, and the night was filled with a hundred terrible sounds – unearthly shrieks, breaking glass, and the cries of the naughty ladies echoing through the alleyways:

'A penny for a kiss o' me ruby-red lips! An' tuppence for a feel o' me elbows!'

Beggars wailed and wept in the gutters, hair thieves stood huddled outside the tattoo parlours and terrifying gangs of gossipers roamed the streets, talking about people behind their backs.

'Outta me way, matey,' growled a fierce-looking sailor, shoving Polly rudely aside as he disappeared in through a crooked doorway. 'I wanna see this bear everyone's goin' on about.'

'Bear?' whispered Polly. Following in after the sailor, she found herself standing in a dingy little tavern.

It was a vile sort of a place, heaving with rough laughter and reeking of sweat and sawdust. Crusty fishing nets hung from the low ceiling, and the tables were packed with red-nosed ruffians boasting about how many men they'd killed and eating anchors for a dare. In one corner a sinister midget sat writing his diary with an old-fashioned feather quill:

September 15th

Woke up. Did some sinister stuff. Killed a man for calling me 'Shorty'. Killed another man just because I felt like it. Did some more sinister stuff. Watched *The Simpsons* .

Trying not to breathe too deeply in case she got drunk, Polly passed through a series of shady backrooms where all manner of illegal entertainments were afoot. Card games, spider-wrestling, rooster-inflating contests – it was all going on. But finally Polly came to the last room of all, a dark dank den tucked away at the very back of the tavern, far from the eyes of decent folk and packed with boisterous sailors, all waiting for the show to begin.

Suddenly a hush descended as a feeble green light was switched on. Polly's eyes widened as Mr Gum stepped out on to a rickety wooden stage, grinning like a haunted shipwreck.

'Good evenin', gentlemen,' said he, 'an' welcome to me brilliant show! An' what a spectacular evenin' of entertainment an' cruelty to animals we got for you tonight! Gentlemen, I present to you the one . . . the only . . . the incredible . . . Mr Funny, the Dancin' Bear!

Bring 'im out, Billy! An' poke 'im in the ribs a bit for a laugh!'

The sailors whooped and screamed as Billy William pushed Padlock roughly into the sickly green spotlight. Then, before Polly's very knees, the poor animal was forced up on to his hind legs and made to shuffle sadly around in cruel iron chains while the sailors hooted and snorted, clapping their hands together and chanting their traditional sea shanty:

Dance for yer supper!

You big ugly tungler!

Dance for yer sailor pals!

An' the wind she blows high an' the wind she blows low

With a wiggle-me-higgle

Me-higgle-me-ho!

With a wiggle-me-higgle

Me-higgle-me-hee!

You hilarious creature

Dance for yer tea!

'So this is what happens to bears lost in the World of Men,' whispered Polly to herself. 'They gets treated like objects to be made fun of! It's an outrage!'

Slowly, slowly, the minutes ticked by. Padlock danced, and Mr Gum sneered, and Billy William passed his greasy cap around, crying, 'Come now, gents! Show yer appreciation for Mr Funty, the Dancin' Bear! Thaaaat's right!' wheedled Billy as the night wore on and the cap grew heavy with golden coins. 'Fill it up with yer riches!'

Polly rubbed her eyes tiredly. Would this hellish spectacle never end? But eventually the last sailor coughed up. The show was finally over. And with the cheers of the crowd still ringing in their ears, the villains bundled Padlock through a back door and out into the misty night.

'Right,' scowled Mr Gum in the dark alleyway behind the tavern. 'Let's see what we got here then. *One bit o' gold in a butcher's cap*,' he counted. *'Two bits o' gold in a butcher's cap . . .'*

While the rascals stood counting their loot in the dancing moonlight, Polly tiptoed over to Padlock, who was slumped exhaustedly against a stack of wooden crates piled higgledy-piggledy upon the slimy cobblestones.

'Nine bits o' gold in a butcher's cap . . . Ten

bits o' gold in a butcher's cap . . . '

Mr Gum's rasping chant mixed with the lapping of the waves like a bad luck dream.

'Padlock,' whispered Polly, 'I let you down back in the town square but I won't never do it 'gain, I swears it!'

'Mmph?' said Padlock weakly. His chest was heaving in and out terribly and Polly was horrified to see how frail he was.

'Come on, boy,' she whispered urgently,

unbuckling the iron chains around the bear's ankles. 'I'm a-gettin' you out of here.'

'Twenty-three bits o' gold in a butcher's cap . . . Twenty-four bits o' gold in a butcher's cap . . . '

'That's the way,' said Polly, as she took Padlock's big brown paw in her little pink hand and together they began to tiptoe down the alley.

'Thirty bits o' gold in a butcher's cap! Well, call me a fatty, me countin' is done! Thirty bits

o' gold, Billy!' said Mr Gum triumphantly. 'Not a bad start but I wants MORE!'

'Well, don't you worry, Mr Gum me old Mr Gum,' laughed Billy William, 'there's plenty other taverns to visit. An' – hold on!' he exclaimed, sniffing with his long thin nose on the wind. 'That smells like a bear escapin'!'

'WHAT?!' roared Mr Gum, his bloodshot eyes a-glintin' an' a-gluntin' in the moonlight. 'I don't believe it!' he roared as he spotted Polly.

'It's that little meddlin' girl an' all! GET 'EM!'

'UUURRF!' With all her strength, Polly pushed desperately at a great pile of barrels, sending them rumbling towards the villains and knocking them flat on their annoying backs. The cap flew from Mr Gum's hand and all the money they'd made went rolling down the alleyway and straight through the open doors of an orphanage.

'Hooray!' cried the orphans, 'now we've got enough money to buy an oven and we can finally eat proper bread instead of this horrible raw dough! Thank you, Mr Gum, you've made our lives much better with your generosity!'

'Shabba me whiskers!' scowled Mr Gum, who hated doing good deeds, even by accident. In a flash the villains were back on their feet and back in the race – but Polly and Padlock had already reached the waterfront.

'Anchors aweigh!' shouted a voice up ahead. Through the fog, Polly could just make out a tall sailing ship with masts and rigging, just like in exciting adventure stories like '**Treasure Island**' or slightly less exciting ones like '**Island**'.

'Anchors aweigh!' shouted the voice again as the ship prepared to leave the docks. Polly glanced back and saw Mr Gum and Billy steaming down the alleyway towards them like the smelliest bowling balls ever born. There was nothing for it but –

'Jump, Padlock, JUMP!' yelled Polly, leaping

on to Padlock's hairy back, and with the last of his strength Padlock done a good one, sailing through the air with his paws stretched out and his fur flying out in every direction.

BEAR NOISE!

He landed heavily on the ship's deck, and by the time Mr Gum and Billy reached the dockside the ship was already pulling away through the murky sloshity waters.

⚓ ⚓ ⚓

'They ain't gettin' away with this!' screamed Mr Gum, jumping on to a rundown little fishing boat called *The Dirty Oyster*. Billy hopped in after him and started up the engine, sending billowing clouds of filthy black smoke into the night air, and off they set in hot pursuit.

But luckily the pursuit wasn't that hot after all, because *The Dirty Oyster* was absolutely

loaded with cans of smuggled beer. In less than ten minutes the villains were completely drunk, completely lost, completely going round in circles, completely shouting at each other and completely and utterly useless.

Polly and Padlock had escaped!

Chapter 6

Captain Brazil

'Hoist the mainsail! Fifty degrees to starboard! Man the rigging!'

A booming voice rang out, seeming to fill the whole world as Polly and Padlock lay shivering on the lurching deck.

'Forty degrees North! Wind the windlass! Lick the ropes!'

The sails flapped and shuddered as the ship began to pick up speed. And from out of the mist stepped a small man in a navy blue uniform, his chest thrust out like a vainglorious acorn.

His grey hair was swept up on top of his head and his eyes were rolling about wildly in their sockets like someone was playing pinball inside his brain.

'What's the meaning of this?' he demanded, strutting over to Polly and Padlock. 'What are you doing aboard my ship? Explain yourselves at once! Actually don't, I can't be bothered to listen. My name's Captain Brazil – welcome aboard the *Nantucket Tickler*!'

🏴 🏴 🏴

Now, Captain Brazil was a very famous sea captain indeed. In his time he had been awarded all sorts of medals, and he had once nearly met someone who knew the Queen. And he had fought in some incredible battles at sea, including *The Incredible Battle At Sea* (1962), *The Incredible Battle At Sea II* (1963), *Revenge of the Incredible Battle At Sea* (1966), *The Incredible Battle At Sea Strikes Back* (1970) and *The Incredible Battle At Sea Gets Married* (1978).

Yes, Captain Brazil was an impressive sight all right, with all those medals on his chest and hardly any soup stains in his hair. But here's the thing. If you look at the dates of those battles, you will see that they were all ages ago, when Captain Brazil had been a young man, fit as a unicorn and twice as real. And now that he was old and grey, some whispered that Captain Brazil had gone mad from too many years at sea and what's more, they were right. He was an absolute CRAZER.

'Right,' Captain Brazil told Polly when the ship was safely out of the docks and in open water, heading into the watery future like only ships know how. 'There's no girls allowed on board the *Nantucket Tickler*, that's a rule. But we do need a cabin boy, so I'm afraid you'll have to do what they always do in exciting sea adventures. You'll have to disguise yourself as a boy to fool me. But watch out. I'm not easily fooled. If I catch any girls onboard, you're in for it!'

'But you already knows I'm a girl,' said Polly in confusion.

'Get disguising, that's an order!' commanded Captain Brazil, his eyes rolling more wildly than ever. 'And that bear's got to go too – although we are looking for a ship's cat,' he hinted.

So Polly and Padlock climbed below decks, and five minutes later they emerged completely transformed. Polly was dressed in shorts and a shirt, with a stick-on moustache made from an old piece of hammock. And she had stuck some triangular ears on Padlock and painted 'MIAOW' on his side in tar.

'Good evenin',' began Polly.

'You sound like a girl,' said Captain Brazil suspiciously. 'Make your voice go deeper.'

'Good evenin', Cap'n,' began Polly again, in as deep and gruff a voice as she could manage. 'My name's Harry Edwards. I been a boy all me life an' I always wee standin' up cos I'm not a girl or nothin'. An' this here's Purrface Mulligan,' she said, pointing to Padlock. 'The bestest pussycat in all London Town. He can catch mice like you wouldn't believe an' he's def'nitely not a bear.'

'Well,' said Captain Brazil happily. 'What a stroke of luck! There we were, looking for a cabin boy and a ship's cat – and now we've found one of each. Welcome aboard! Now run off, you scallywags, and go and ask Cook for some dinner.'

But as soon as the two of them were out of sight, Captain Brazil rubbed his chin thoughtfully.

'Hmm,' he frowned, 'there's something not quite right about this "Harry Edwards" fellow. He talks like a boy and he walks like a boy – but I've got my suspicions. And as for that "cat" of his, well, I'm just not sure he's a cat at all. I shall have to keep a very close eye on those two. No one fools Captain Brazil!'

What an absolute CRAZER!

Chapter 7
Life at Sea

Man the rigging! Scrub the decks! Hoist the mainsail! Do something with a rope! Fry the bacon! Eat the bacon! Say, "mmm, that was nice bacon"! Play the accordion! Stop playing the accordion! Sit around doing nothing for a bit! Do the crossword! Trip over a bucket and go "ouch!" Climb the mast pretending to look out for whales, but really just have a crafty snooze! Do something else with a rope!'

Each morning Captain Brazil would issue his commands, and each morning the ship's men would scuttle around doing everything he said. For although he was as mad as a dandelion, Captain Brazil's men loved him like a brother, especially one of the crew called Longlegs Henderson, who actually *was* his brother.

And all things considered, life aboard the *Nantucket Tickler* was really quite pleasant. Polly was every bit as good as a real cabin boy and she soon made herself very useful, polishing the captain's nose, mending old sails with needle and thread, and fetching supplies from below deck for Cook. The only problem came when she was told to give the ship's rail a new lick of paint.

'What's this?' thundered Captain Brazil, examining Polly's handiwork. She had painted the rail a lovely shade of bright pink and decorated it with little red hearts, glitter and stickers of ponies.

'You're not really a girl in disguise are you, Harry Edwards?' said the captain suspiciously.

'Oh, no,' replied Polly in her gruffest voice, kicking herself for having made such a stupid mistake. 'Course not, Cap'n.'

'Well, you'd better not be,' muttered the little man, leaning in so close that Polly could see

her own face reflected in his well polished nose.
'No one makes a fool of Captain Brazil!'

👃 👃 👃

Still, the rest of the crew suspected nothing and
they were generally quite kind to Polly. The First
Mate, a jolly, white-bearded fellow by the name of
Nimpy Windowmash, had taken a particular
liking to the new cabin boy and he spent hours
teaching Polly all the tricks o' the sea – how to

tell what direction you were going in by just having a bit of a guess, what 'hoist the mainsail' actually means (nothing at all) and how to find out how cold the water is by pushing someone into the water and asking them how cold it is.

And as for Padlock, or 'Purrface Mulligan' as the sailors knew him, he wasn't really a very good ship's cat and he never once did manage to catch a mouse – but he didn't seem to be quite so sad these days. Perhaps the sea air was doing him some good.

And so the *Nantucket Tickler* sailed on, through fair skies of blue and through squally storms, through seas as calm as a new-born handkerchief and seas as angry as a heavy metal band stuck in a lift. Round the Cape of Good Hope they sailed, into the Indian Ocean and on past Curly Michael, the naughty sea serpent who lives off the coast of Madagascar, terrorising passing ships with his boring stories about kelp. And as the days stretched into weeks, Polly began to feel that things were going to work out fine.

'You know,' she told Padlock one warm tropical evening, as the dolphins blew on their trumpets and the sun sank slowly in the West, 'everythin' turned out pretty good. I dunno where this ship's headin' but I reckons we're soon gonna gets you back to the Kingdom of the Beasters, where you can roam wild an' free an' hairy once more. An' best of all, we done completely escaped from Mr Gum,' she continued. 'Mark my words, Padders, he won't be botherin' us no more.'

Chapter 8

Two Men in a Boat

Mr Gum stood on the oily deck of *The Dirty Oyster*, scowling at everything in sight. Not that there was much to scowl at – just a load of water, a bit of sky and a line in between called the 'horizon' which God had put there to keep the sky from getting wet.

'Shabba me whiskers,' scowled Mr Gum for the thousandth time since they'd left Lamonic Bibber. He and Billy had been adrift at sea for weeks now and they were practically dead of hunger, thirst and general scruffiness. All the beer had run out long ago, the engine was smashed to bits from a game they'd invented called 'Let's Smash Up The Engine' and they were both covered from head to toe with sunburn, mosquito bites and verrucas.

'Shabba me whiskers,' scowled Mr Gum for the thousand and one-th time since they'd left Lamonic Bibber. 'I'm completely sick of all this floatin'-around-miles-away-from-home business. What a bother it all is!'

'An' I'm sick of bein' bitten by things,' complained Billy, rubbing a wound on his shoulder where some plankton had attacked him.

'Yeah,' grimaced Mr Gum, 'but the worst thing is how hungry I'm a-gettin'. Ain't you got no more dried entrails, Billy?'

'Sorry, Mr Gum, me old lifejacket,' said Billy, 'you scoffed the last one this mornin'. We could try catchin' some fish,' he suggested. 'Look, there's a fishin' rod an' everythin'.'

'Nah, I can't be bothered with all that, it looks like too much hard work,' growled Mr Gum, snapping the fishing rod over his knee and chucking the pieces into the ocean.

'Now what we gonna do?' whined Billy. 'We're gonna starve to death at this rate.'

'Sorry, Billy, me old roast dinner, but there's nothin' else for it,' said Mr Gum. 'I'm gonna have to eat you to stay alive. Chop off yer leg for us, will ya?'

Billy was just about to start sawing into his manky old leg, when all of a sudden he sighted an island ahead, a-glimmerin' and a-shimmerin' 'neath the blazing South Pacific sun.

'Land! Land!' he shouted, 'we're saved!'

And together the villains danced round and round the deck, whooping and roaring with filthy delight as the island drew nearer.

Chapter 9

Discovered!

Night time and the *Nantucket Tickler* sailed softly on the clear calm waters, watched over by a full moon which hung in the sky like a big silver fruit pastille. Down below decks, Polly awoke with the strange feeling that something was wrong. Quiet as an avocado, she slid from her hammock, opened the cabin door and climbed up on deck.

'Easy does it,' whispered Polly to herself as she prowled around, being extra careful to keep to the shadows. She knew the punishment for being caught on deck after dark – tickling, and lots of it. Oh, it didn't sound so bad, and at first it was even quite fun. But only last week she had seen Captain Brazil tickle a man so hard that both his lungs had flown out his nostrils, it was horrible.

And now, very faintly, Polly could hear laughter and accordion music coming from the far end of the deck, behind one of those massive funnels you always get on ships, no one even knows what they're for. As her ears grew accustomed to the dark, she began to make out the words of a sea shanty –

Dance for yer supper!

You big ugly tungler!

Dance for yer sailor pals!

And all at once Polly knew what she would find behind the massive funnel.

'Oh, Padlock,' she groaned, 'they've got you a-dancin' again for their gigglin' fun. You poor creature,' she exclaimed as she raced along the deck, 'even here at sea you isn't free of the terrible World of Men an' their wicked ways!'

An' the wind she blows high an' the wind she blows low

With a wiggle-me-higgle

Me-higgle-me-ho!

With a wiggle-me-higgle

Me-higgle-me-hee!

The music and singing grew louder as Polly neared the funnel, until –

'OI! SAILORS!' she yelled, bursting upon the scene she had feared most. There was

Padlock, up on his hind legs, jigging along sadly to the accordion music and crying, as all around the sailors stood jeering and poking him with their famous Sailors' Sticks.

'You jus' stops these cruelties right now!' scolded Polly, throwing herself into the middle of the ring.

'Look, it's little Harry Edwards, the cabin boy!' sneered a mean old fellow called Brendan Jawsnapper, whose muscular arms were covered all over with tattoos of fists and ambulances. 'What do you mean by breakin' up our fun? We only wanna see the pussycat dance!'

'Yeah, he's the best dancin' cat what we ever had on this ship,' agreed someone else.

'Well, I'm afraid he's not here for your prancin' amusements!' said Polly fiercely. 'You jus' leave Padlock – I mean, Purrface Mulligan – alone!'

'That does it,' growled Brendan Jawsnapper,

and punching himself twice in the face (once for practice and once because he enjoyed it) he launched himself into the ring, snarling like a greasy-haired hurricane.

'MMPH,' growled Padlock, stepping forward to protect Polly, his claws glinting menacingly in the moonlight.

'Blood! Blood! Blood!' chanted the sailors eagerly. 'Blood on the water tonight!'

Brendan Jawsnapper and Padlock circled

each other slowly, two contestants trapped in a deadly game of Man Against Bear Disguised As Pussycat . . .

But before anyone could land the first blow, Captain Brazil came striding into the ring, woken from his slumbers by all the ruckus on deck.

'Stop these shenanigans right now!' he bellowed. 'Hoist the mainsail! Fifty degrees North! I won't tolerate this sort of nonsense on my ship! Who's responsible?'

'It was Harry Edwards,' said Brendan Jawsnapper. 'He started it, Cap'n!'

'Yeah,' the others chimed in, 'it was Edwards and his moggy!'

'I've had just about enough of this,' said Captain Brazil, grabbing Padlock by the ear, only to have it come off in his hand. And with the removal of the brilliant cat disguise, Captain Brazil had finally discovered the bare truth of the bear truth.

'By King Neptune's underwater train set!' he roared. 'By the wooden sharks of the Mahogany Sea! This isn't a cat at all, it's a BEAR! And wait just a minute,' he exclaimed, lunging forward and whipping Polly's fake moustache from her face.

'Aha!' cried Captain Brazil triumphantly. 'You're not a boy at all, you're a GIRL! Thought you could fool me, did you? Well, you're in for it now!'

'B-but don't you remembers?' pleaded Polly as the captain advanced on her, rolling up his sleeve. 'You was the one what told us to do them 'mazin' disguises in the first place!'

'Why on earth would I tell you to do a thing like that?' said Captain Brazil in bemusement, his eyes rolling around like ice skaters in his head. 'That would be insane! Now prepare to be tickled 'til your lungs fly out of your nostrils!'

'No, Cap'n! You can't!' cried good-hearted Nimpy Windowmash, the First Mate. 'She's as good as any boy! Have mercy, Cap'n, please!'

'Hmm,' said Captain Brazil, stroking his leg thoughtfully. 'Nimpy, you are a good First Mate and your name makes me laugh. Plus you once rescued me from being eaten by a prawn. Perhaps I should listen to you.

'Very well,' he continued, 'I will not tickle her – but she will still have to be punished. Men!' boomed Captain Brazil, 'let it be known that at sunrise, she and the bear will be put on a plank and set adrift on the ocean blue!'

Chapter 10

She and the Bear are Put on a Plank and Set Adrift on the Ocean Blue

*I*t was three minutes to sunrise. Polly and Padlock sat shivering upon a wooden plank no bigger than a mattress as it bobbed gently upon the waves. Far above on the deck of the *Nantucket Tickler*, Captain Brazil and his men stood gazing down at them. Some of the men were shaking their heads sadly. Nimpy Windowmash was crying. Brendan Jawsnapper was leaning over the rail, making rude faces and trying to gob phlegm on to Padlock's head.

'Harry Edwards and Purrface Mulligan,' said Captain Brazil gravely. 'You thought you could make a fool of me, but you yourselves are the fools, you fools. Three minutes from now the sun will rise, and I will cut the rope which tethers your plank to this ship. Actually I can't be bothered to wait, I'll just do it now.'

SCHWICK!

With one firm swipe of his cutlass, Captain Brazil slashed through the rope.

'NO!' shouted Polly.

'MMPH!' said Padlock.

A great wave bore down, sweeping up the plank and carrying it far from the ship in a single watery heartbeat. Salt water stung Polly's eyes and mingled with the tears rolling down Padlock's face.

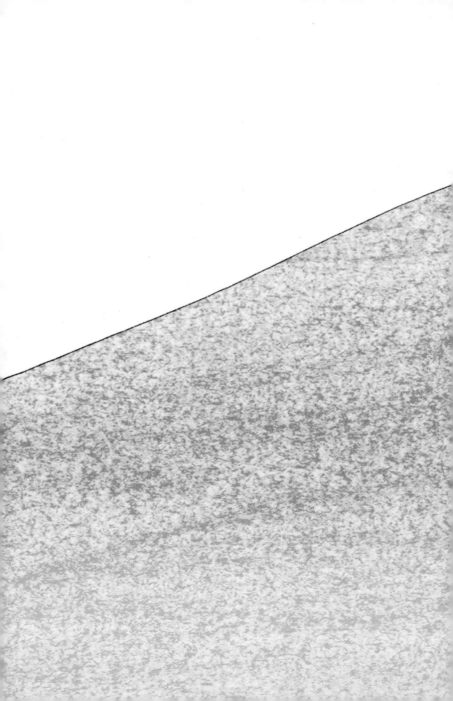

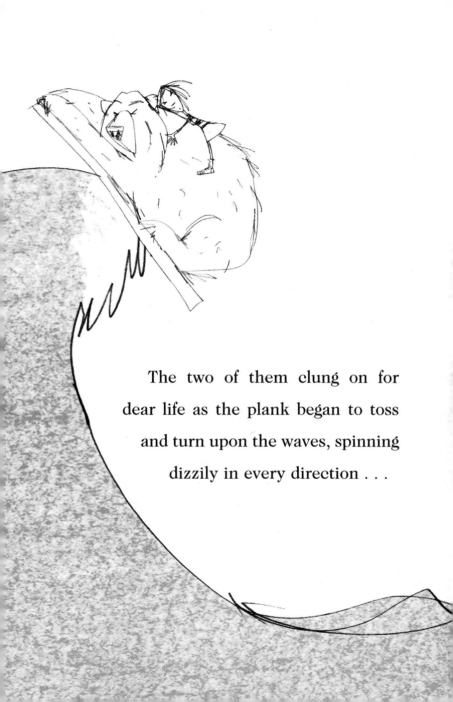

The two of them clung on for
dear life as the plank began to toss
and turn upon the waves, spinning
dizzily in every direction . . .

SPLOOOOOOOOSSSSSSHHHH.

'NOOOOOO!' yelled Polly. 'You can't do this to us, Cap'n!'

But it had already been done.

Gradually the plank was carried further and further away from the ship.

Soon the *Nantucket Tickler* was only a pinprick on the horizon.

And then it was lost from view entirely.

SHHHHHWWWWWOOOOOOSSSSSH.

SWWWWWOOOOOOOSSSSH.

SWWWSSSSSShhhhhhhh.

Adrift on the ocean wave, with only a bear for company.

There was nothing to do.

There was nothing to see.

Just the big blue sea.

And the big blue sky.

Stretching out as far as the eye could see . . .

Just the big blue sea.

Big blue sky.

Big blue nothing.

And poor little Polly and Padlock caught in the middle of it all, floating through the Universe on a plank no bigger than a mattress.

Swwwwwshshssh.

'HELP!' called Polly. But who was listening?

'GRRRMPH!' wailed Padlock. But who would answer?

Not the sky.

Not the sea.

Not the clouds.

Adrift, adrift on the big fat blue.

SWWWSSSSShhhhhhhh.

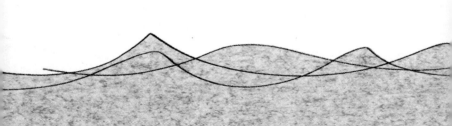

'Blimey, I'm getting thin,' said Padlock, running his paws over his ribcage.

WWWWWWWHHHEEEEEEEEEEEEEEEEEEEEEEE٫BÔING٫

Thirst and hunger.

Thirst and hunger.

Polly was starting to lose her mind.

Was Padlock really talking or had she only imagined it?

SWWWSSSSShhhhhhhh.

Hundreds of **Crunchy Little Leopards** floated by in a postman's hat, laughing and splashing each other for fun.

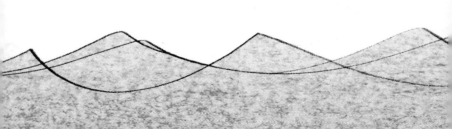

'Look at me,' said Padlock, taking off his head and playing football with it. 'Ha ha ha, hee hee hee!'

SWWWSSSSShhhhhhhh.

SWWWSSSSShhhhhhhh.

A fish zoomed straight up out of the water and went soaring into the sky where it exploded into a shower of cackling seahorses that all looked like Billy William the Third. A mackerel with the face of Mr Gum swam by, watching 'Bag of Sticks' on a waterproof TV set.

'Shabba me dorsal fin,' muttered the mackerel. 'Who'd've thought bein' a mackerel would be such a bother?'

SWWWWWOOOOOOSSSSH.

The world was turning upside down.

Polly tasted salt water, saw the sky tumbling around her. Padlock kept turning into Captain Brazil's nose and back again.

Was Polly dreaming? Was she awake? Was she asleep? Was she somewhere in between?

She looked down and saw her hands had turned into bear's paws.

WHEEEEEEEEEEEEEEEEEEEEEEEEEEEEEEEEEEEE! BOING!

She was losing her mind.

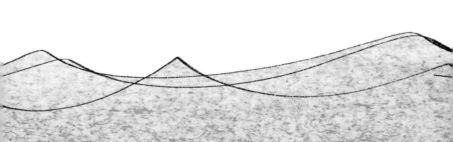

Ssssswwwwwshhhhh.

Ssswwhsssh.

The big blue sea.

Ssswwhsssh.

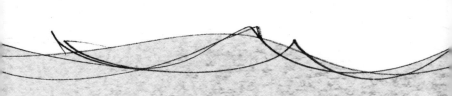

Pictures drifted through Polly's head. Padlock was holding a toy balloon. Holding a funny red balloon on a funny yellow string, la la la!

'Can I have a go?' said Polly, but Padlock had gone.

Where was he?

He was climbing up the string, la la la!

Climbing up the string and disappearing up through the air like a furry dream . . .

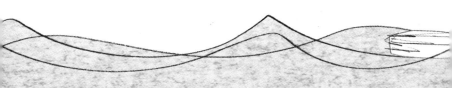

Look up, Polly, look up!

'UP HERE, POLLY!' called a voice from above. 'LOOK UP!'

'What? What you on about, mysterious voice?' said Polly sleepily.

'LOOK UP IN THE SKY!'

'Oh, the sky!' laughed Polly. 'Padlock disappeared up there, you know,' she giggled.

'Grab hold of the ROPE, Polly!' shouted the voice.

Slowly Polly looked around. She was still all alone.

Blue sea.
Blue sky.
A yellow rope.
Blue sky –
Hold on.

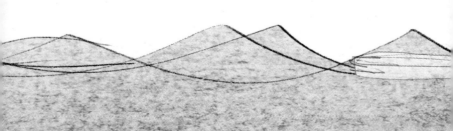

A yellow rope?

Polly's eyes followed the rope upwards into the air and there it was. Not a toy balloon after all! But a splendid red hot-air balloon with

FLAVOURS OF DISCOVERY

painted on the side in letters of green and gold.

'Mr Ripples, sir!' croaked Polly in disbelief. 'What on earth are you doin' here?'

'Come on, Polly!' yelled Jonathan Ripples.

'Padlock's already made it,' he said, gesturing towards the bear standing at his side in the basket. 'Now it's your turn. Climb up!'

'I don't thinks I can!' called Polly, 'I'm too weak!'

But already she had taken hold of the rope and already – slowly, slowly – she was hauling herself up, Jonathan Ripples urging her on every step of the way.

'That's it, that's it! You're doing ever so well!'

Every muscle in Polly's body ached agonisingly as she climbed, and once she glanced down and saw a family of sharks laying out a dinner table with knives and forks, waiting for her to fall –

But was Polly the type of girl to give up? Yes, she was, I mean, no, she wasn't. Up she pulled herself, up, up through the sky like a dinosaur fighting its way back from extinction.

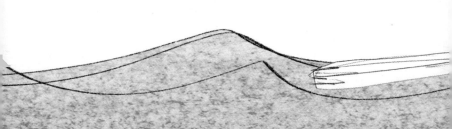

Up, up she went. Until, eventually, she was at the top of the rope and Jonathan Ripples was helping her into the crowded basket. What a tight squeeze it was! But she was safe.

'Oh, Mr Ripples, sir,' said Polly, half-collapsing against Padlock's furry legs. 'I can't . . . I can't thanks you enough . . .'

'Shh,' said Jonathan Ripples kindly. 'Eat first,

then we'll talk. Try some sushi,' he suggested, offering Polly a tray of raw fish and rice. 'It's the latest snack I discovered, over in Japan.'

'But . . . but . . . however did you done find us, Mr Ripples, sir?' said Polly, nibbling at the horrid delicacy.

'Well, it's the strangest thing,' said Jonathan Ripples as he bit into a vegetable samosa he'd found on a park bench in India. 'I was flying north in search of my latest snack, but last night

I had the most peculiar dream. There was a little boy, laughing in a sea of colours, and he said,

"Hello, Jonathan Ripples. I like your hot-air balloon. Now, finding snacks is very important, but I have an even more important job for you to do. Tomorrow you must turn your balloon all the way around and find some friends of mine who are in trouble. Bye for now!"

'So this morning I turned the balloon around and there you were,' said Jonathan Ripples. 'It's probably just a coincidence,' he laughed, 'after all, it was only a dream.'

But Polly knew better.

'No, large sir,' she said solemnly, 'you was destined to finds us. For last night you was a-visited in your sleeps by none other than the Spirit of the Rainbow.'

'The Spirit of the Rainbow?' chuckled

Jonathan Ripples, crunching into a burrito he'd discovered down Mexico way. 'Never heard of him. Sorry, Polly, but I think you've gone a little bit crazy in the head from too long at sea!'

Chapter 11
To the Island

*O*h, those days sailing not through the seas but through the bright blue skies in Jonathan Ripples' balloon! They were beautiful days, magical days, wonderful, mystical, zam-zistical days! And the nights were pretty zam-zistical too, only a bit darker.

'How I loves it up here,' said Polly, as they flashed and flurried through the laughing, hoopling clouds. 'It's like a dream!'

'But it's even better than a dream,' chuckled Jonathan Ripples, 'because we've got all those delicious snacks I collected before I rescued you. Fancy another potato 'n' donkey yum-yum all the way from China?'

'Um, not just now, thanks,' said Polly, who didn't really like the potato 'n' donkey yum-yums very much. They were a bit too potato-ey for her.

Even Padlock began to look a little happier during this time. He would spend entire days with his paws up on the edge of the basket, gazing down at the sparkling sea as it sped past below, or pulling funny faces to amuse the albatrosses and gulls that wheeled in dizzying arcs around the balloon.

'Why, I do believes we're seein' the real Padlock at last,' smiled Polly. 'I never seen him

enjoyin' life like this, Mr Ripples, sir. His fur's a-startin' to grow back an' everythin'.'

But each evening as the sun went down and the sky blazed orange and gold and red, Polly would find her thoughts turning to Lamonic Bibber, the town she knew and called Lamonic Bibber.

'I wonder what Friday O'Leary's up to right

now,' she would sigh wistfully. 'I haven't seen him for ages.'

Or, 'I does miss Old Granny. Her an' her sherry-lovin' ways! An' what about little Alan Taylor? I wonder how he's gettin' on at Saint Pterodactyl's?'

'When's we a-gonna be back in Lamonic Bibber, Mr Ripples, sir?' asked Polly one night as she prepared to bed down next to Padlock, who always kept her warm and safe and smelling a bit like a bear.

'If my calculations are correct, we'll be there tomorrow morning,' replied Jonathan Ripples, studying his map and sucking on a kiwi smoothie he'd picked up over in New Zealand. And that night Polly went to sleep with a contented smile on her face, dreaming that she was back home on Boaster's Hill with Jake the dog, pretending he was a horse or a spaceship.

☁ ☁ ☁

But the next morning, Jonathan Ripples looked worried.

'I'm afraid my calculations weren't correct, after all. Look, Polly,' he said, pointing to an orange blob on his map. 'I thought this was England, but it turned out to be a bit of chicken tikka I spilt the other night.'

'Then where do you thinks we are?' said Polly.

'Well, according to my *new* calculations, which are based on countries rather than food stains,' replied Jonathan Ripples, 'we've been going in the wrong direction for days. We're somewhere over the South Pacific, which is miles from anywhere. I think we'd better land at the next island we see and stock up on snacks.'

So Polly kept a lookout for land and later that morning she saw a small island, sitting in the middle of the ocean like a crouton in a very very

very very VERY big bowl of fish soup. It was covered in lush tropical green with golden-white sandy beaches at the edges, and it looked very inviting indeed.

'Land!' shouted Polly. 'Let's land!'

'Just think of all the snacks just waiting to be discovered down there,' said Jonathan Ripples as he steered the craft skilfully towards the island.

'Easy does it, easy does it,' he muttered in concentration, sweat pouring down his smooth chubby face. 'Polly, haul that rope in, would you? We don't want it getting tangled up in the treetops.'

Polly watched in admiration as J.R. brought them closer to the dazzling sands.

'Mmph,' said Padlock, bouncing up and down with excitement. The wicker basket began to rock from side to side. 'Mmph, MMPH!'

'Control him, can't you, Polly! He's steering us off course!' cried Jonathan Ripples frantically as the balloon descended.

'Padders, Padders!' urged Polly, 'calm it down, boy, calm it down!'

'MMPH!' said Padlock. 'MMPH!!'

Padlock's jumps were getting worse than ever

and the basket was tilting over to one side . . .

SHHHHOOOOOOFFF!

A great gust of wind caught them from below
and the balloon was lifted far over the beach and
hurled into the dark green treetops.

POIK! MEMP! SKRUP!

WHARK! TWIG!

The world was a tumble of green, red, brown . . . They crashed through the branches, snacks flying everywhere – goulash, hot dogs, Pad Thai noodles . . . A deadly popadom whizzed past Polly's ear and sliced into a tree trunk, cutting it clean in two.

'Polly!' yelled Jonathan Ripples desperately as the two of them were thrown from the basket towards the forest floor. 'GRAB HOLD OF MY FLAB! GRAB HOLD OF MY FLAAAAAAB!'

And then everything went dark.

☆ ☆ ☆

It was early afternoon when Polly came to her senses. She was covered in scratches and bits of potato 'n' donkey yum-yum, but otherwise she seemed to be unharmed.

Something soft must have cushioned her fall – and looking down she saw what it was. She was lying on Jonathan Ripples' stomach.

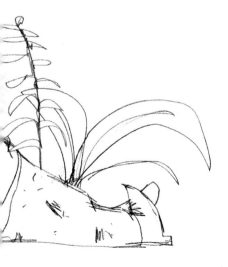

'Oh, you big brave guzzler,' cried Polly, climbing down and kneeling by his side. 'Are you all right, sir?'

'Got to . . . land the balloon . . . ' moaned Jonathan Ripples, his eyes squeezed tight shut in concentration. 'Keep that . . . bear . . . under control or we'll . . . crash!'

'We already done crashed, sir,' said Polly gently, and opening his eyes Jonathan Ripples saw the truth of it. His lovely red balloon, which he had worked so hard to build with his own podgy hands, hung raggedly from the treetops, all tattered and torn as it dangled on the breeze like a wilted ant.

'What about . . . the . . . snacks?' he gasped. 'Tell me the . . . snacks are . . . all right, Polly.'

Polly looked away, unable to meet Jonathan Ripples' hopeful, pleading eyes.

'I'm afraid . . . well, I'm afraid the snacks didn't make it,' said Polly quietly. 'I'm sorry, sir.'

'NNOOOOOOOOOOOOOOOOOOOOOOO!'

Jonathan Ripples' roar of anguish echoed through the forest, shaking the trees and ferns to their roots. But after some time the fat man was able to pull himself together.

'Well, snacks will come and snacks will go, I suppose,' he said, getting up and dusting himself off. 'The important thing is that we're all right.'

'Yes,' said Polly anxiously, 'but Mr Ripples, Mr Ripples, what 'bout Padlock? He's nowheres to be seen!'

Chapter 12
The Hunt for Padlock

'Oh, hold on, there he is,' said Polly. 'Over by that leaf. I didn't see him there for a moment.'

Chapter 13
Exploring the Island

'Well, everyone's basically all right,' said Jonathan Ripples cheerfully. 'Let's see what this island's got to offer in the way of snacks.'

Yes, it was an official Jonathan Ripples Snack Discovering Expedition, or 'JRSDE' for short.

So off they set through the rainforest, making their way beneath the low-hanging vines and creepers. From time to time, Jonathan Ripples would stop to investigate the plants and rocks for any snacks that might be hiding there, but Polly was far more interested in the natural beauty of the island. She had never seen anything like it.

'Why, it's like some sorts of paradise,' she marvelled, gazing around the lush rainforest, unspoiled by Man or Shopping Centre. Insects the size of birds buzzed all around, birds as small as bees darted through her eyelashes and the colours were so dazzling she thought her brains would go mental with happiness.

'An' jus' look at Padlock!' laughed Polly joyfully. 'He loves it here an' he's doin' somersaults to prove it!'

It was true. Padlock was a-bouncin' and a-boundin' ahead of them like the world's furriest gymnastics guy. And when Polly saw him roaming so wild and free and hairy she realised the truth of it.

'Why, this must be the Kingdom of the Beasters at last!' she said in wonder. 'That's what's makin' Padlock so happy an' filled with power an' playtime!'

Giggling with glee, Polly went skipping after

her friend, and there in a forest clearing she found him, rolling around in the huge violet flowers, rubbing his back in pleasure against the tree trunks and pooing wherever he flipping well felt like. He had never looked more like a proper fat shaggy rumble-me-tumble sort of a roly-poly flip-flap-flopper of a big brown bear than he did at that moment. And the sun it shone down and the butterflies bibbled and the day was as bright as Cleopatra's nail varnish. And Padlock and Polly stood there in the clearing together, gazing into one another's eyes with love and hope for the future. For they had done it. Padlock had finally come home – home to the Kingdom of the Beasts where he belonged.

It was a magical moment and the only thing that spoilt it was when Mr Gum and Billy William jumped out from behind a vine and whacked Padlock around the head with a big rotten log crawling with giant woodlice.

'Ha ha!' laughed Mr Gum. His horrible skin was red with sunburn, his horrible beard was red with just being red to begin with, and there was evil written all over his face. He had written it there that morning in biro.

'Not so proud an' strong now, are ya?' he yelled at Padlock, who lay cowering on the ground in fright.

'Ha ha!' laughed Billy, putting his foot on Padlock's head and pretending like he was going to squash it. 'He knows who's the boss – us!'

'You good-for-nothin' pair of hofflers! What on earth you doin' here?' demanded Polly furiously.

'It was all part of me amazin' genius plan,'

boasted Mr Gum. 'See, we decided to sail to this island on purpose. We knew you'd turn up eventually with the bear – it was just a matter of waitin' for you.'

'Actually we just sort of landed here by accident,' admitted Billy. 'To be honest, we've been drunk most of the time an' – OW!'

'Shut up,' said Mr Gum, whacking Billy round the head with the log. 'Now, little girl, take one step closer an' I'll finish off your precious

"Padlock" once an' for all. Billy, you repaired our boat engine yet?'

'Yeah,' said Billy William. *The Dirty Oyster*'s back in business, Gummy, me old paint bucket.'

'Right then,' said Mr Gum, prodding Padlock in the back with a stick. 'Let's get off this stinkin' island an' go an' make our fortune with Mr Funny, the Dancin' Bear.'

'I hates you, Mr Gum!' shouted Polly, 'an' to be quite franks I don't much care for you neither, Billy William! He's NOT Mr Funny, an' he's NOT a dancin' bear! He's a wonderful animal with dignity an' pride an' pretty hazel eyes an' he don't belongs with you, he belongs here!'

'So you don't like to see a bear dancin'?' grinned Mr Gum. 'Well, bad luck, Girly McSwirly – you're gonna get one last performance before we go.'

And then the villains started up with that terrible shanty they loved so well:

Dance for yer supper!

You big ugly tungler!

Dance for old Gummy an' Bill!

An' the wind she blows high an' the wind

she blows low –

But Padlock wouldn't dance.

He had had enough.

'Dance!' shouted Mr Gum wildly. 'Dance, you filthy old flea-bear, dance!'

But no.

Padlock's doleful hazel eyes looked deep into Polly's and in that moment he seemed to find his greatest strength yet. Not the sort of strength that helps you lift a sack of babies over your head in a Baby-Lifting Competition, but the sort of strength that comes deep from the inside. The sort of strength that tells the world, *'I am a bear, not a dancing clown! And I am proud like the wind, and free like the wind, and wild like the wind! Hey, maybe I am the wind! No, hold on, I'm a bear, yes, I'm definitely a bear! And you may poke me with sharp sticks and call me a tungler, but you will never again make me live in the World of Men!'*

And Padlock threw back his head and oh, boy, he HOWLED, a noise so mournful and long and rich with ancient animal power that even Mr Gum drew back in alarm.

'HRRRRRRRRRRRRRRRRRRh

WLWLWLLLLLLLwww!

The beautiful, lonely sound carried to every corner of that island, calling to the creatures that lay hidden there, waiting for the signal of a brother in pain. And slowly, gradually, hundreds of eyes began appearing among the trees and ferns. Hundreds of pairs of eyes, blinking ominously all around the forest clearing.

'What's goin' on?' whimpered Mr Gum. 'I don't likes it, I don't likes it one bit!'

Chapter 14
The Kingdom of the Beasts

Slowly a figure emerged from the trees. It was a bear.

Slowly a second figure emerged from the trees.

It was another bear.

Slowly a third figure emerged from the trees.

It was Jonathan Ripples.

'Hello, Polly,' he said. 'Have you found any snack – ooh, what's happening here?'

'Shh,' said Polly, 'it's the Kingdom of the Beasters, come to full power at last.'

One by one, more and more bears stepped out from among the trees, until very soon Mr Gum and Billy were completely surrounded by a circle of the big brown creatures, all grinning and growling and showing their sharp white teeth.

'What we gonna do?' wibbed the villains, clutching on to each other. 'They're gonna rip us apart an' suck the marrow out our bones, whatever marrow is!'

But now all sorts of other animals were

beginning to show themselves as the news spread: apes, mice, bees, antelopes, parrots, toucans, wild horses, even wilder horses, completely livid horses, bright tree frogs so poisonous they kept killing themselves by accident, orang-utans, blue lizards, elephants, tigers, a rhino called Larry Bennett, stag beetles, beetle stags, giant centipedes, a little dog riding on a monkey and tons of other tropical weirdies you've never even heard of –

all of them came trotting or flying or slithering up to join the party. A blue whale came running out of the ocean just to have a look, and a piglet sent a note to say he was terribly sorry he couldn't make it but he was busy being eaten by a python.

And then, once all the animals were assembled, Padlock rose to his full height. And very slowly and deliberately he began to stomp his paws upon the ground.

STOMP.

STOMP.

STOMP.

STOMP.

One by one the other animals joined in, stomping their feet or swishing their tails in time, and what a racket they raised that day, my friends! You've never heard anything like it, or maybe you have, who knows what you get up to in your spare time? Anyway, what a racket! And the way those animals stared at the villains! You would have sworn they were trying to tell them something.

'Oh, if only we poor animals could talk,' exclaimed a large red parrot, flapping his wings in despair, 'then we could tell you what was on our minds.'

But Jonathan Ripples had already figured it out.

'Pardon me,' he said to the villains, 'but I think . . . um . . . well, I think the animals want you to *dance* for them.'

At this the animals threw back their heads and shrieked and stomped even harder than before.

'WHAT?!' shouted Mr Gum in horror. 'I ain't no fancy dancin' man!'

'Me neither,' moaned Billy. 'I ain't flappin' around like no disco boogie-boy for some stupid bunch of wildlife!'

But at this the animals began to growl and bare their teeth, stomping closer and closer and louder and louder, raising their hooves and paws dangerously.

There was nothing for it. Shaking with rage and embarrassment, Mr Gum and Billy lifted up their clodhopping old hobnail boots and, their faces redder than ever, they began to dance.

'They're makin' us into their fun,' sobbed

Billy as he capered.

'What if they never let us stop?' whimpered Mr Gum, doing a twirl.

Never had such a sight been seen on that island. The animals stamped and brayed and nodded their heads, bellowing and roaring and squawking and buzzing and hooting. And indeed it did seem as if the beasts might carry on forever – but Polly was shaking her head. She just couldn't stand to see another person in trouble, even if that person happened to be Mr Gum and Billy William the Third.

'Oh, Padders, this isn't right!' cried Polly, hopping into the circle alongside the astonished villains and throwing her arms around the big old bear. 'If you treats Mr Gum an' Billy like they done treated you, then you're no better than them! An' the Kingdom of the Beasters will become like the World of Men, full of bad revenges an' hatreds an' makin' people dance. Please, I begs you! Remember you are Beasters, not Men, an' stop this dreadful punishment at once!'

Did Padlock understand Polly's speech? Well, not exactly. He didn't understand the words, of course. But animals are clever animals and they can sense all sorts of things that you and I have no way of knowing about, like emotions and feelings and dog food. So yes. When he gazed into Polly's pleading eyes, Padlock sensed the truth of the matter and truly he was ashamed.

'Mmph,' he said softly, looking around the forest clearing at the animals he had called to that leafy place. 'Mmph.'

All at once the other animals understood and they too were ashamed of what they had become. They ceased their excited frenzy at once, and one by one they crept back into their shadows to resume their peaceful lives of eating each other.

'Quick,' said Mr Gum, seizing the chance.

'Let's get out of here, Billy!'

Away they raced through the forest, away from the shining natural world of the animals, a world they could never understand or learn to stroke gently. Arriving at the beach, they fired up *The Dirty Oyster* and they were off. That was the last that was ever heard of them in the South Pacific Islands, and where they ended up only time will tell.

Chapter 15

The Spirit
of the Rainbow?

'Well,' said Jonathan Ripples, who had finally discovered a snack on the island – a really small coconut that tasted like sick. 'It's all over. The time has come to return to Lamonic Bibber at last.'

'But how can we, Mr Ripples, sir? Our ballooner's all damaged up beyond repair,' said Polly.

'Oh, yes, I'd forgotten about that,' said Jonathan Ripples glumly. 'Whatever are we going to do?'

But just then Padlock's ears pricked up and he started dashing through the forest, turning somersaults as he went.

'Why, he's gone quite mad,' laughed Polly as

she and Jonathan Ripples followed him down to the beach. But there upon the shining white sands stood the hot-air balloon, fully repaired and as good as new, and surrounded by hundreds and hundreds of happy laughing creatures, frolicking in the sunshine and having their races.

'Oh, my LORD! The animals have fixed the balloon!' shouted Jonathan Ripples, falling over in disbelief and getting sand down his trousers.

'Not the animals,' laughed Polly, seeing that the basket was loaded with enough fruit chews to last them the entire trip back home. 'You know, Mr Ripples, sir, I think the Spirit of the Rainbow's been helpin' us out again.'

'Oh, Polly,' smiled Jonathan Ripples. 'Not that nonsense again! Just who is this Spirit of the Rainbow character supposed to be, anyway?'

'Why, don't you knows, sir?' said Polly seriously. 'He's a marvellous little boy what's probbly also a supernatural Force for Good an' he often comes to our aid when we needs him most.'

'Well, where is he then?' said Jonathan Ripples, scratching his head and looking up and down the beach.

'He's everywhere,' said Polly firmly. 'He's all around us at all times, if only we could jus' open up our hearts to see him. Except when his mum calls him an' he has to go home for his tea, that is.'

'Really, Polly,' frowned Jonathan Ripples as

he tried to make sense of it all. It was all most peculiar – but he had to admit that the balloon really was mended.

Well, maybe, just maybe she's right, thought Jonathan Ripples to himself – and for just one moment, he thought he could make out a small shape playing in the sparkling waves, laughing like a schoolboy while calypso music played somewhere far off. And though Jonathan Ripples never spoke of that moment to anyone, he cherished it all his life. And often, as he was going downstairs for a midnight feast back in his house in Lamonic Bibber, he would remember that moment. His hand would pause on the fridge door and he would think, *Perhaps I don't need a snack just now, after all.* And he would go back upstairs to his enormous bed and sleep like the happy bouncing baby he had once been, all those years ago before the hunger got him.

It was early evening and the first shadows were starting to crawl across the sand. The waves lapped gently at the shore like a mother's lullaby and far out to sea a flock of herrings wheeled through the sky, singing their mournful song. It was time to depart.

'I'm gonna miss you, Padlock,' sobbed Polly, throwing her arms around her friend's thick glossy neck and gazing deeply into his beautiful hazel peepers. 'You made me as proud as a go-kart an' I won't never forgets you, though I knows I won't never see you ever again. Cos just as you was a stranger in our world, this island isn't for the likes of me. I hopes you have a nice long life, Padders, an' maybe you'll think of me sometimes an' smile.'

Then Padlock bit her head off. Not really, but it would have been funny if he had.

'Goodbye, Padlock,' said Jonathan Ripples as the big red balloon began to rise. Soon they were high above the island and Padlock was just a dot on the golden-white sands below. But he was a happy dot. A healthy dot. A dot roaming wild and free and hairy like nature intended.

Goodbye, Padlock, goodbye!

Chapter 16
Home Again

'And that's how it all done happened,' said Polly as she sat with her friends upon Boaster's Hill a few weeks later. The sun was shining, a warm breeze was blowing and there wasn't a wasp in the sky. It was good to be back home.

'What an extraordinary tale,' said Mrs Lovely. 'And that awful ship! I bet you're glad to be back on dry land.'

'I am indeeds,' said Polly. 'I did quite like bein' a cabin boy – but next time I wouldn't choose the *Nantucket Tickler* to sails on, that's for sure.'

'I'm glad to hear it,' said Friday O'Leary, who was lying in the grass pretending to be a daisy to see what it felt like. 'That Captain Brazil fellow sounds like an absolute CRAZER!'

'How I wish I could have seen the Kingdom of the Beasts with my own eyes,' said Alan Taylor, the gingerbread headmaster, as he played and scampered in Jake the dog's fur. 'It sounds amazing.'

'Oh, it was,' said Jonathan Ripples happily. 'And best of all, we even managed to stop off in China on the way back and pick up some more potato 'n' donkey yum-yums. Anyone fancy one?'

But no one did, not even Jake the dog, who gave an indignant 'woof!' as if to say, 'haven't you got any nice bones instead, you big overweight human?' and everyone laughed, not because they were making fun of Jake or anything, just because it's fun when dogs bark. Unless they're about to attack you, that is.

And there we shall leave Polly and her friends, laughing and barking and pretending to be a daisy. For it is time once again to say goodbye. Goodbye, Polly! Goodbye, Alan Taylor! Goodbye, Friday and Mrs Lovely! Goodbye, Mr Ripples, sir! Goodbye, Jake! Goodbye, Martin Launderette! Sorry you weren't in this story, maybe you'll be in the next one, who knows? Goodbye, everyone, goodbye!

THE END

MAPS
&
SNACKS

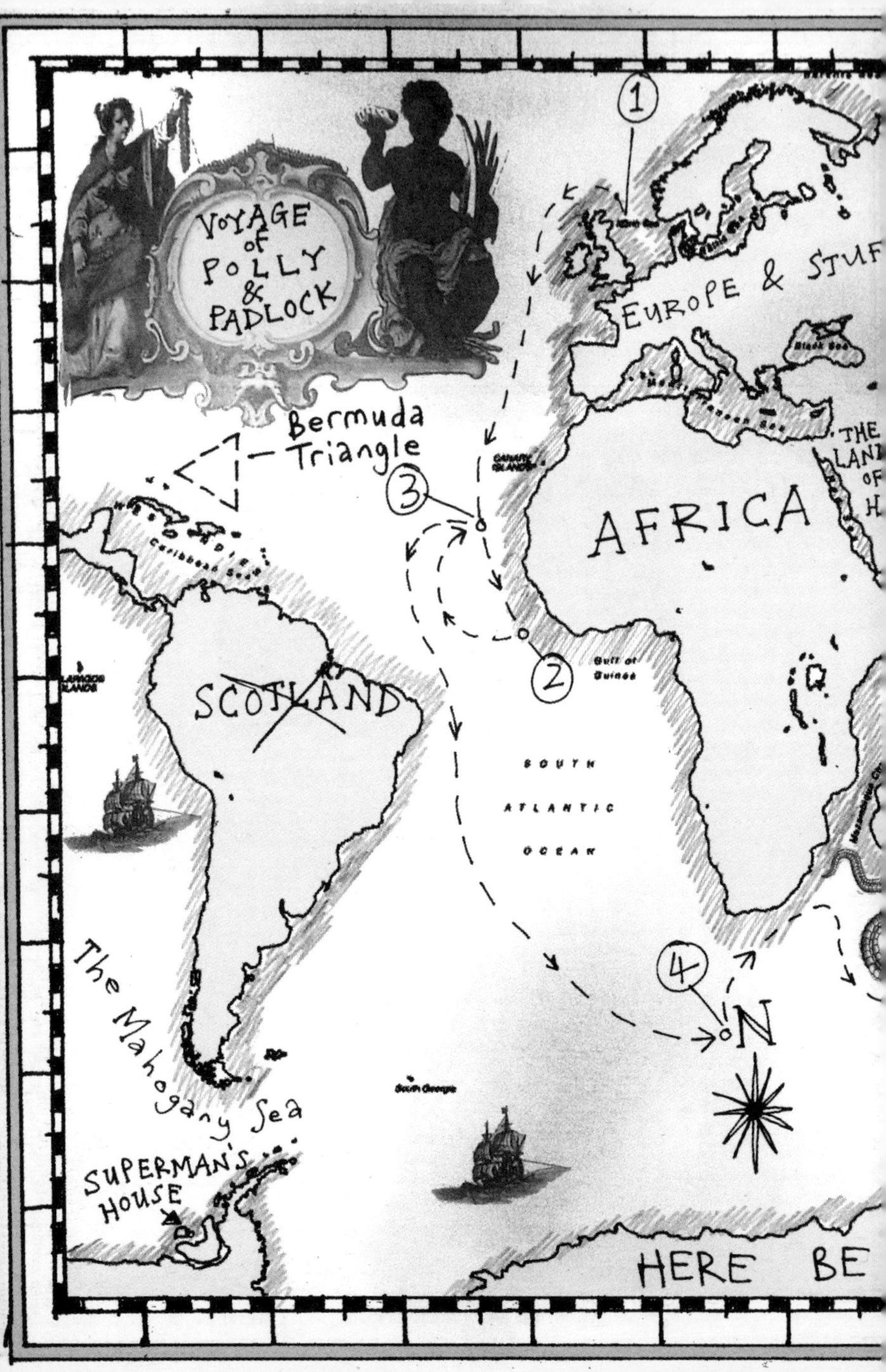

VOYAGE of POLLY & PADLOCK
1
EUROPE & STUF
Black Sea
THE LAN OF H
Bermuda Triangle
3
CANARY ISLANDS
AFRICA
Caribbean Sea
2
Gulf of Guinea
SCOTLAND
SOUTH ATLANTIC OCEAN
The Mahogany Sea
4
N
South Georgia
SUPERMAN'S HOUSE
HERE BE

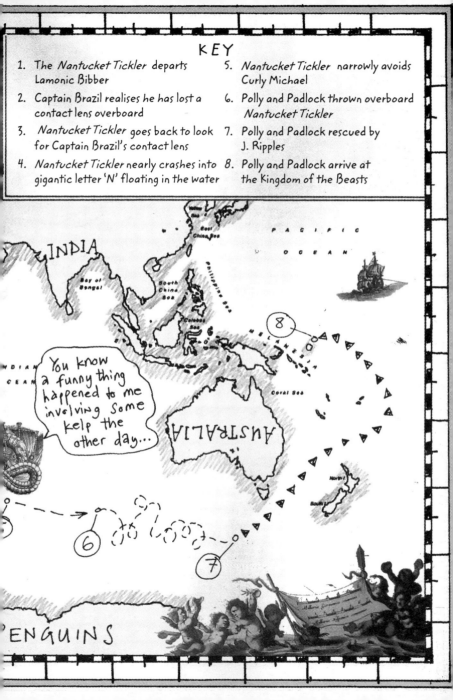

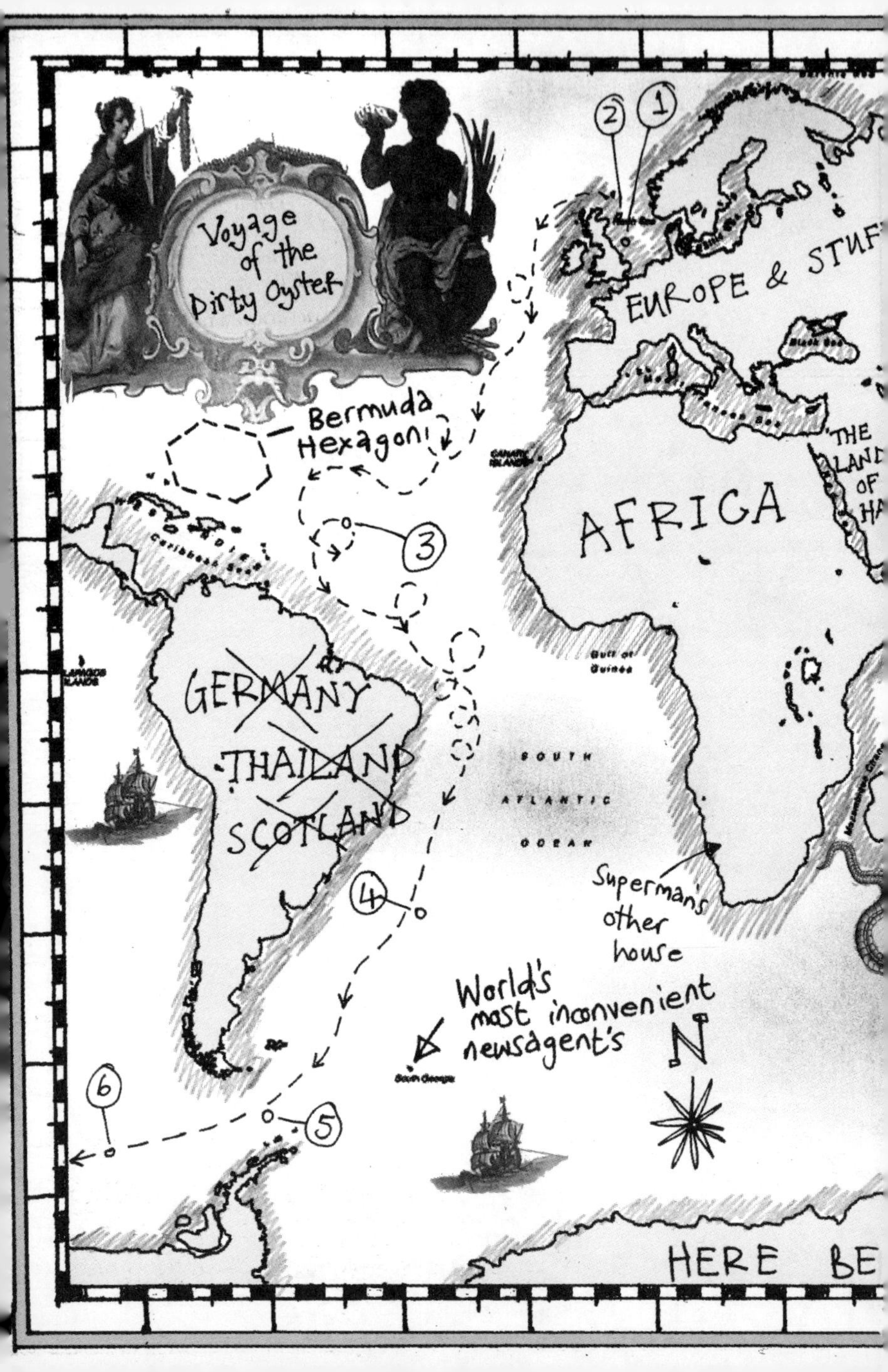

Voyage of the Dirty Oyster
1
2
EUROPE & STUF
Black Sea
Bermuda Hexagon!
THE LAND OF HA
AFRICA
3
Caribbean Sea
Gulf of Guinea
GERMANY
THAILAND
SCOTLAND
SOUTH ATLANTIC OCEAN
4
Superman's other house
World's most inconvenient newsagent's
South Georgia
N
6
5
HERE BE

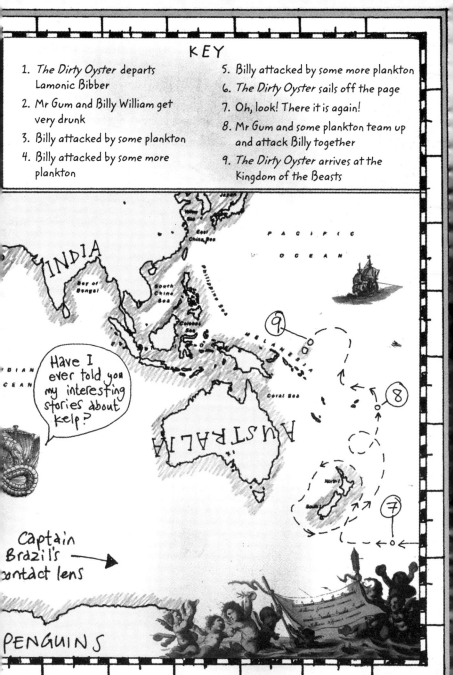

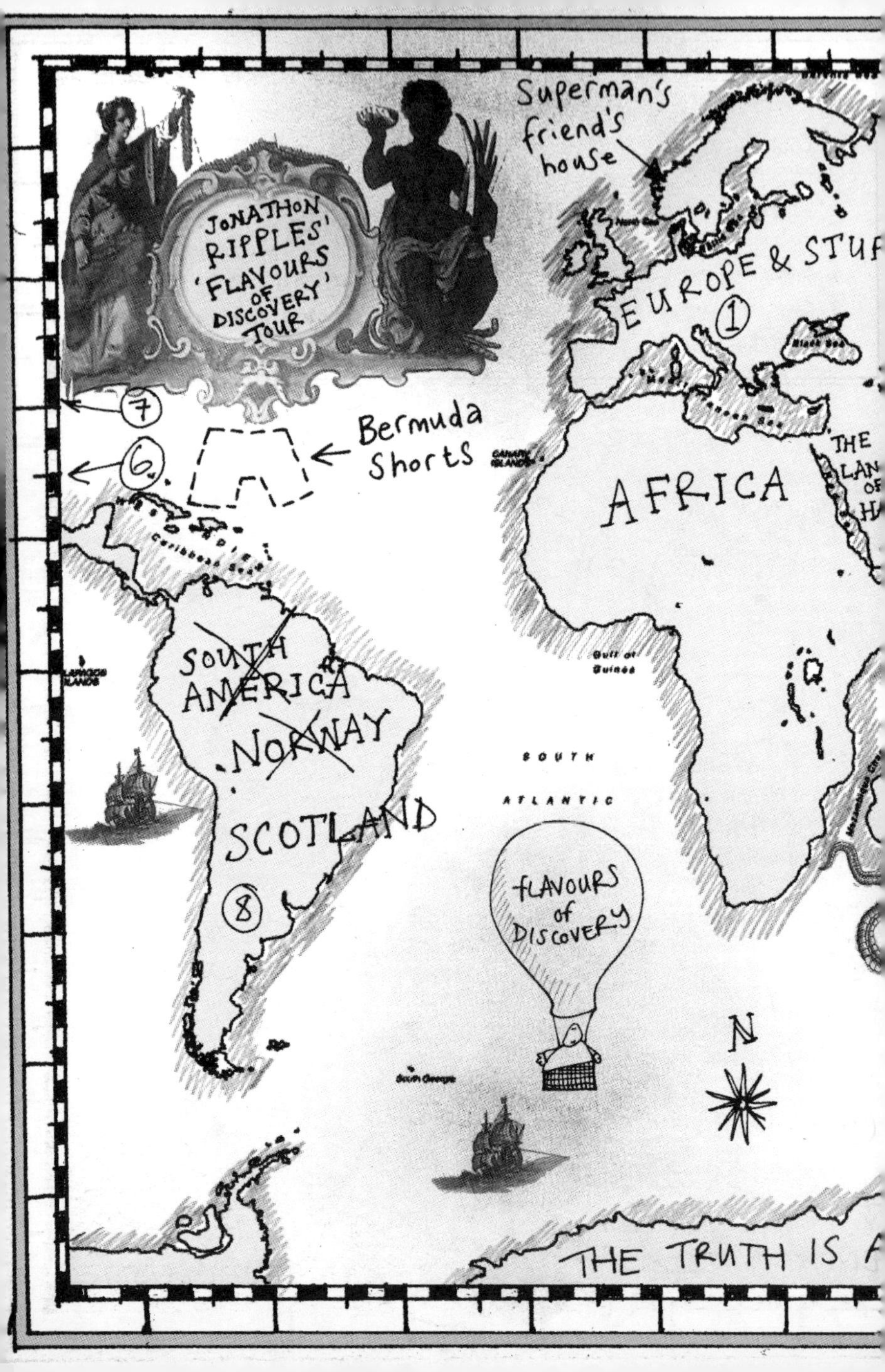
JONATHON RIPPLES' 'FLAVOURS OF DISCOVERY' TOUR
Superman's friend's house
EUROPE & STUF
1
7
6
Bermuda Shorts
THE LAN OF H
AFRICA
SOUTH AMERICA
NORWAY
SCOTLAND
8
SOUTH ATLANTIC
FLAVOURS of DISCOVERY
N
THE TRUTH IS A

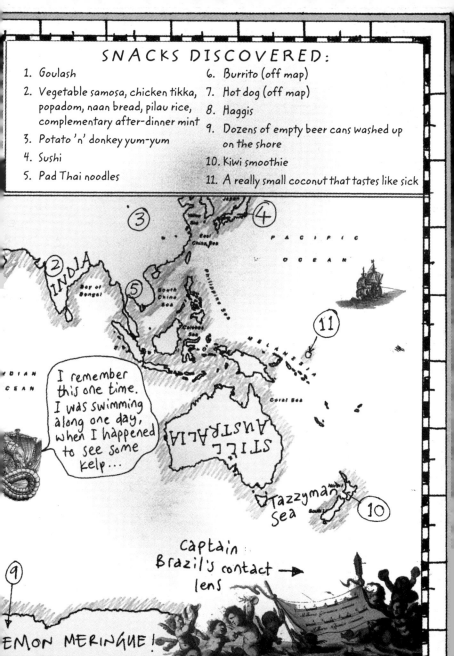

About the Author

Andy Stanton lives in North London. He studied English at Oxford but they kicked him out. He has been a film script reader, a cartoonist, an NHS lackey and lots of other things. He has many interests, but best of all he likes cartoons, books and music (even jazz). One day he'd like to live in New York or Berlin or one of those places because he's got fantasies of bohemia. His favourite expression is 'I live my life as I see fit' and his favourite word is 'snorkel'. This is his fifth book.

About the Illustrator

David Tazzyman lives in South London with his girlfriend, Melanie, and their son, Stanley. He grew up in Leicester, studied illustration at Manchester Metropolitan University and then travelled around Asia for three years before moving to London in 1997. He likes football, cricket, biscuits, music and drawing. He still dislikes celery.

Have you read all the MR GUM books?

They're WELL BRILLIANT!

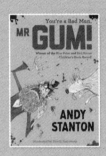

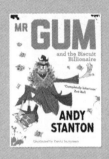

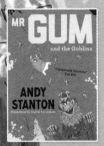

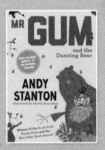

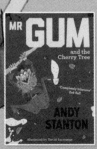

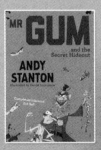

THOUGHT **MR GUM** WAS WEIRD?
WELL, JUST WAIT TIL YOU MEET . . .

THE PANINIS

OF POMPEII

VESUVIUS →

← CAECILIUS

DON'T ASK

SLAVIUS

A FROG

BARKUS
WOOFERINICUM

FILIUS

ANOTHER FROG

More mind-bending craziness from

ANDY STANTON

Illustrated by Sholto Walker

IT'S
TOGA-LLY
TERRIFIC!

Surf the Net in Style! at . . .

mrgum.co.uk

Why do exercise and healthy outdoors pursuits
when you can sit all hunched up in front of a tiny
computer screen, laughing your little face off
at the 82% official, all-bonkers
OFFICIAL MR GUM OFFICIAL WEBSITE?!

Yes, no lie, it's true! The OFFICIAL
MR GUM OFFICIAL WEBSITE features:

Things!

Games!

Photos of the author with beard and without!

Videos including an episode of Bag of Sticks!

Loud noises!

Words like 'YANKLE', 'BLITTLER' and 'FLOINK'!

Crafty Tom – the Tyrannosaurus rex
with a heart of gold!*

You'll never need to go outdoors again!

*Actual website may not include Crafty Tom

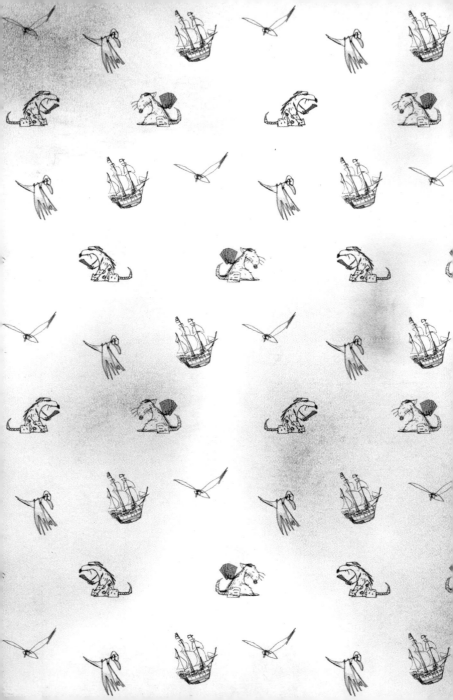